Ladybird  Readers

The Magic Porridge Pot

Series Editor: Sorrel Pitts
Text adapted by Sorrel Pitts
Illustrated by Laura Barella

LADYBIRD BOOKS

UK | USA | Canada | Ireland | Australia
India | New Zealand | South Africa

Ladybird Books is part of the Penguin Random House group of companies
whose addresses can be found at global.penguinrandomhouse.com.
www.penguin.co.uk   www.puffin.co.uk   www.ladybird.com

Penguin
Random House
UK

First published 2016
005

Printed in China

A CIP catalogue record for this book is available from the British Library

ISBN: 978–0–241–25406–6

Penguin Random House is committed to a
sustainable future for our business, our readers
and our planet. This book is made from Forest
Stewardship Council® certified paper.

Ladybird Readers

The Magic Porridge Pot

Picture words

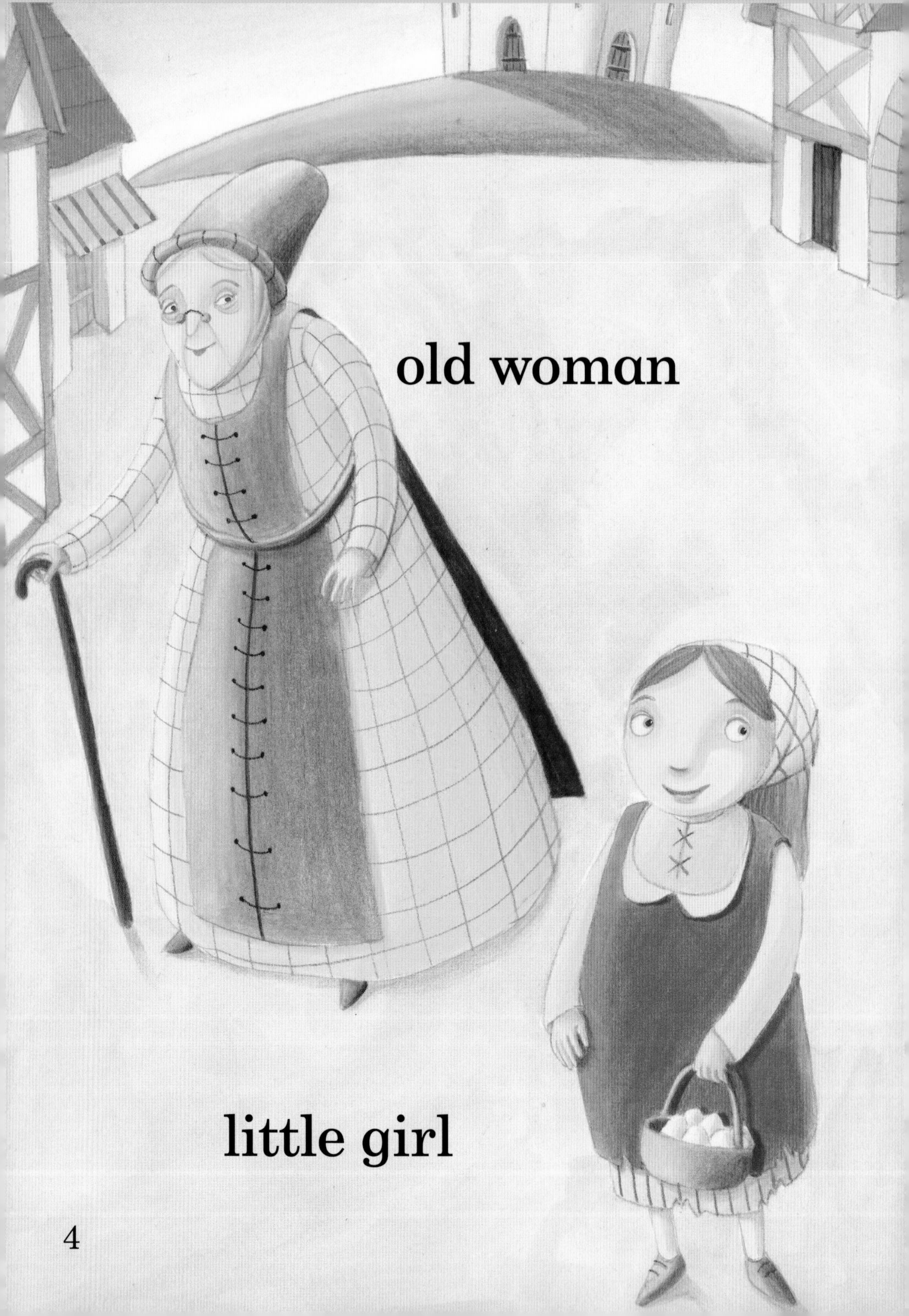

old woman

little girl

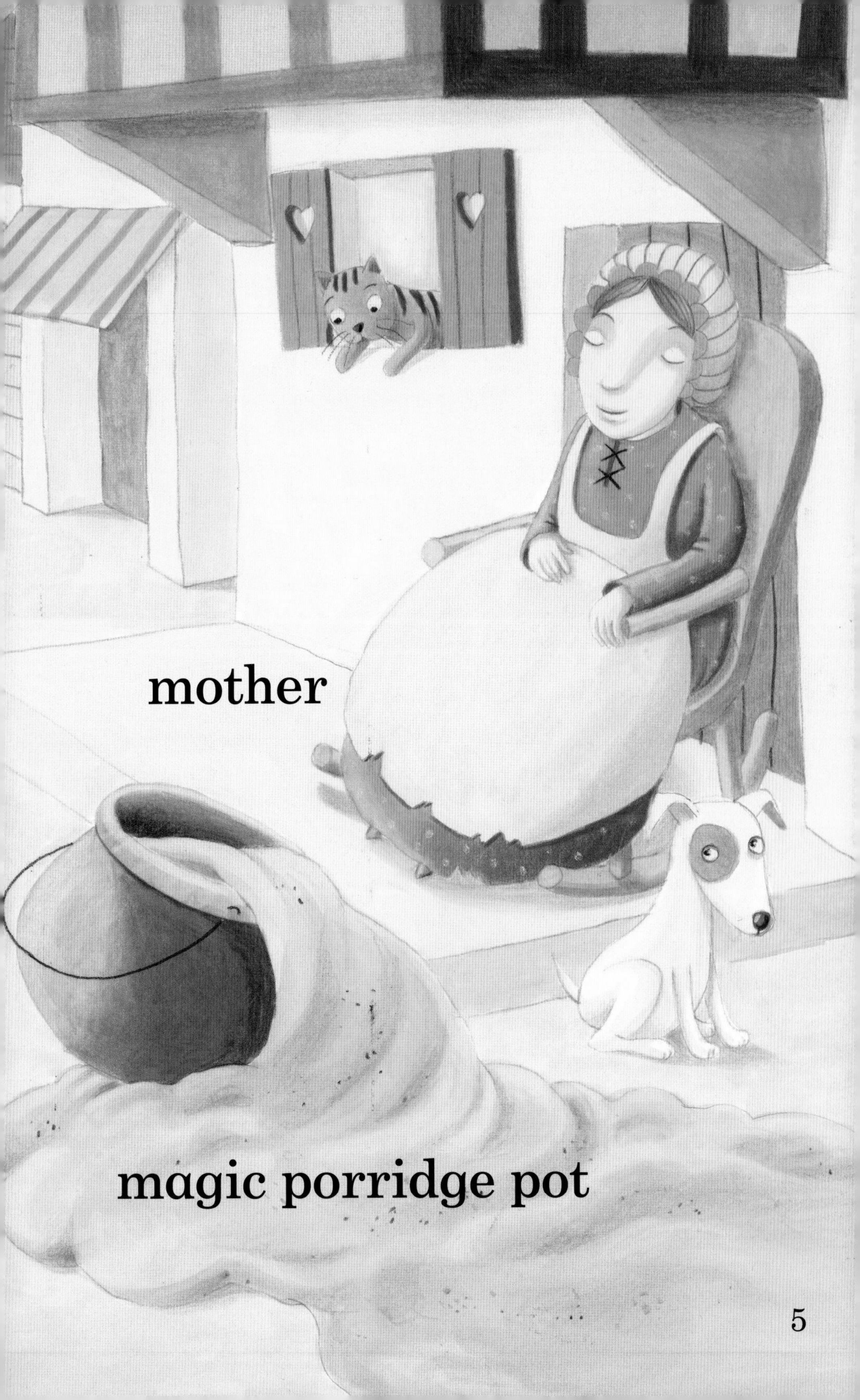

mother

magic porridge pot

One day, a little girl
meets an old woman.

The old woman gives
her a magic porridge pot.

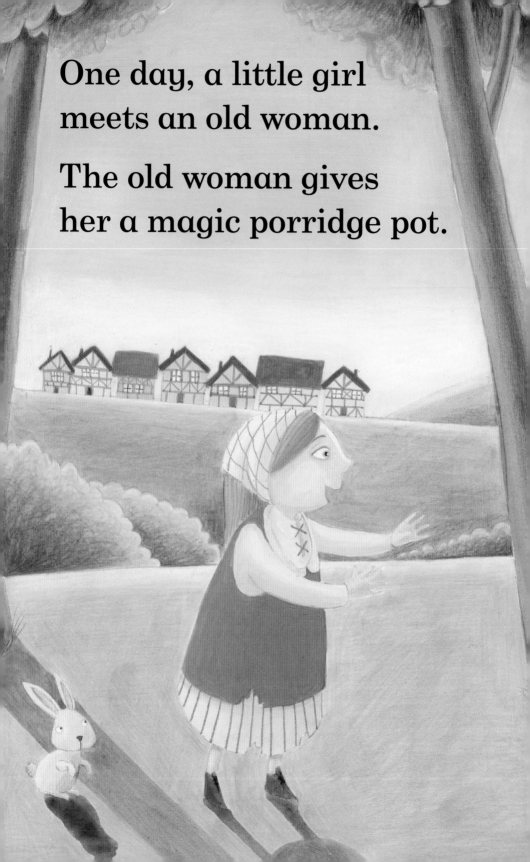

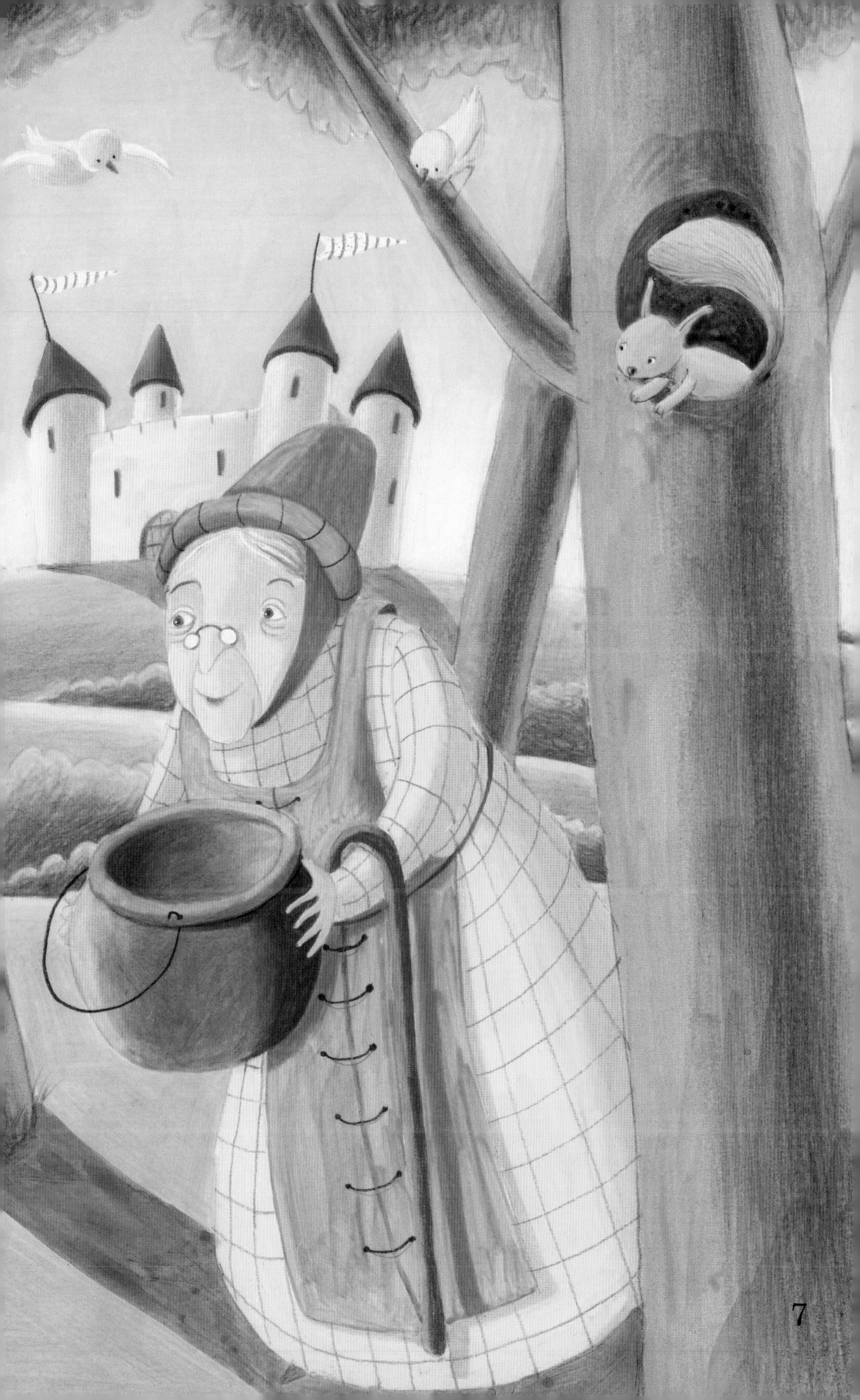

"Cook, little pot, cook," says the old woman.

And the little pot cooks some porridge.

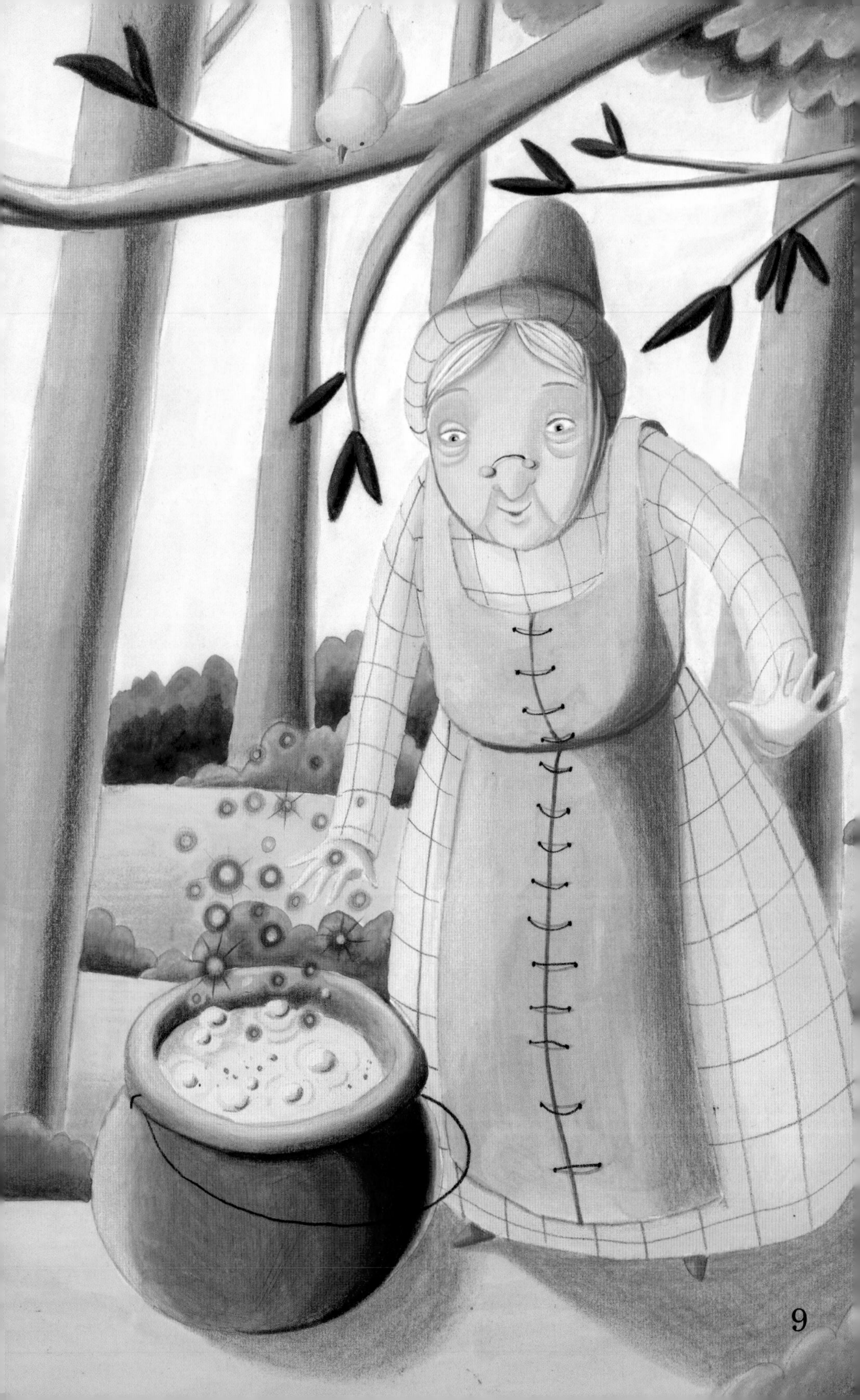

"Stop, little pot, stop," says the old woman.

And the little pot stops cooking.

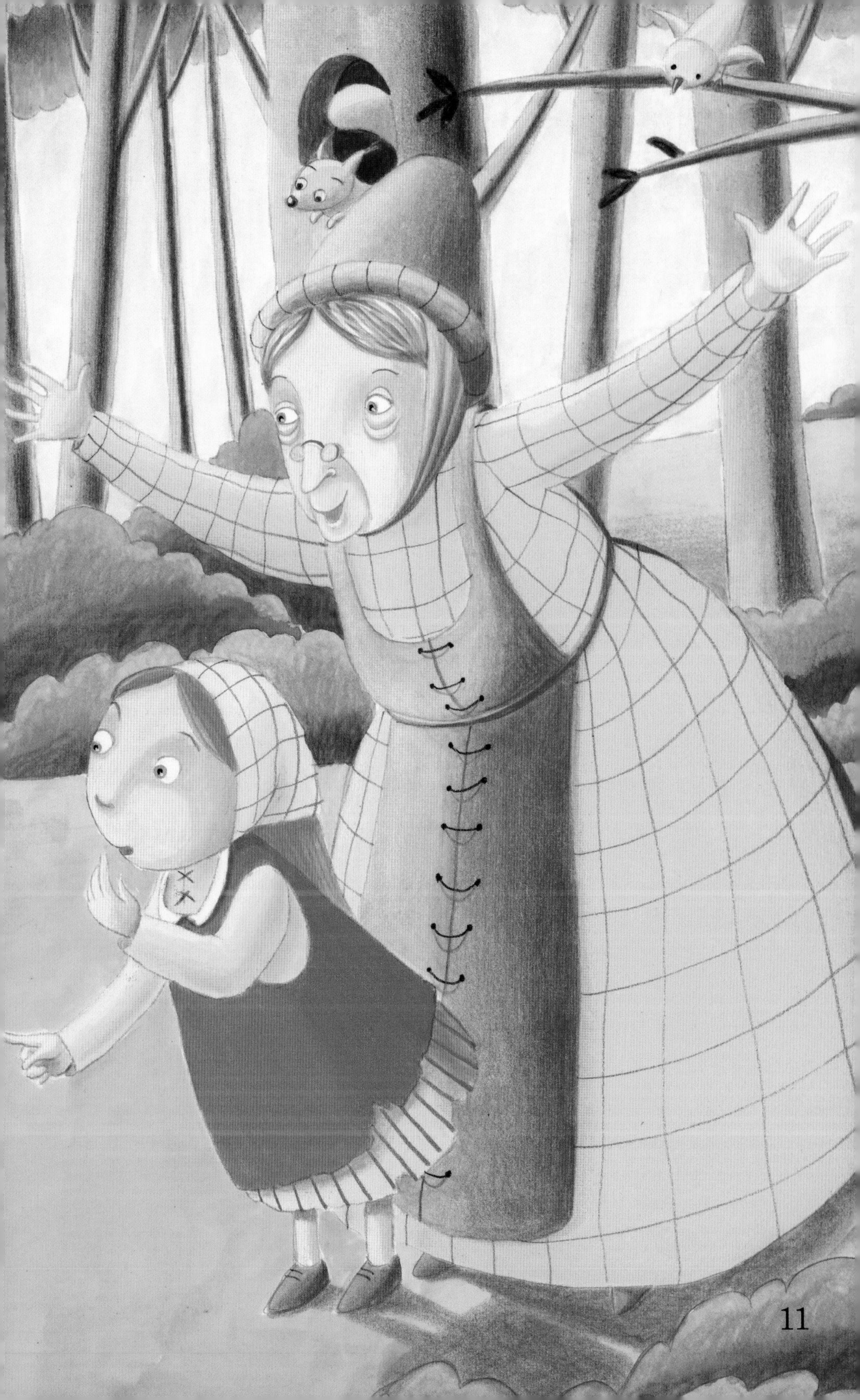

The little girl takes the
magic porridge pot
to her mother.

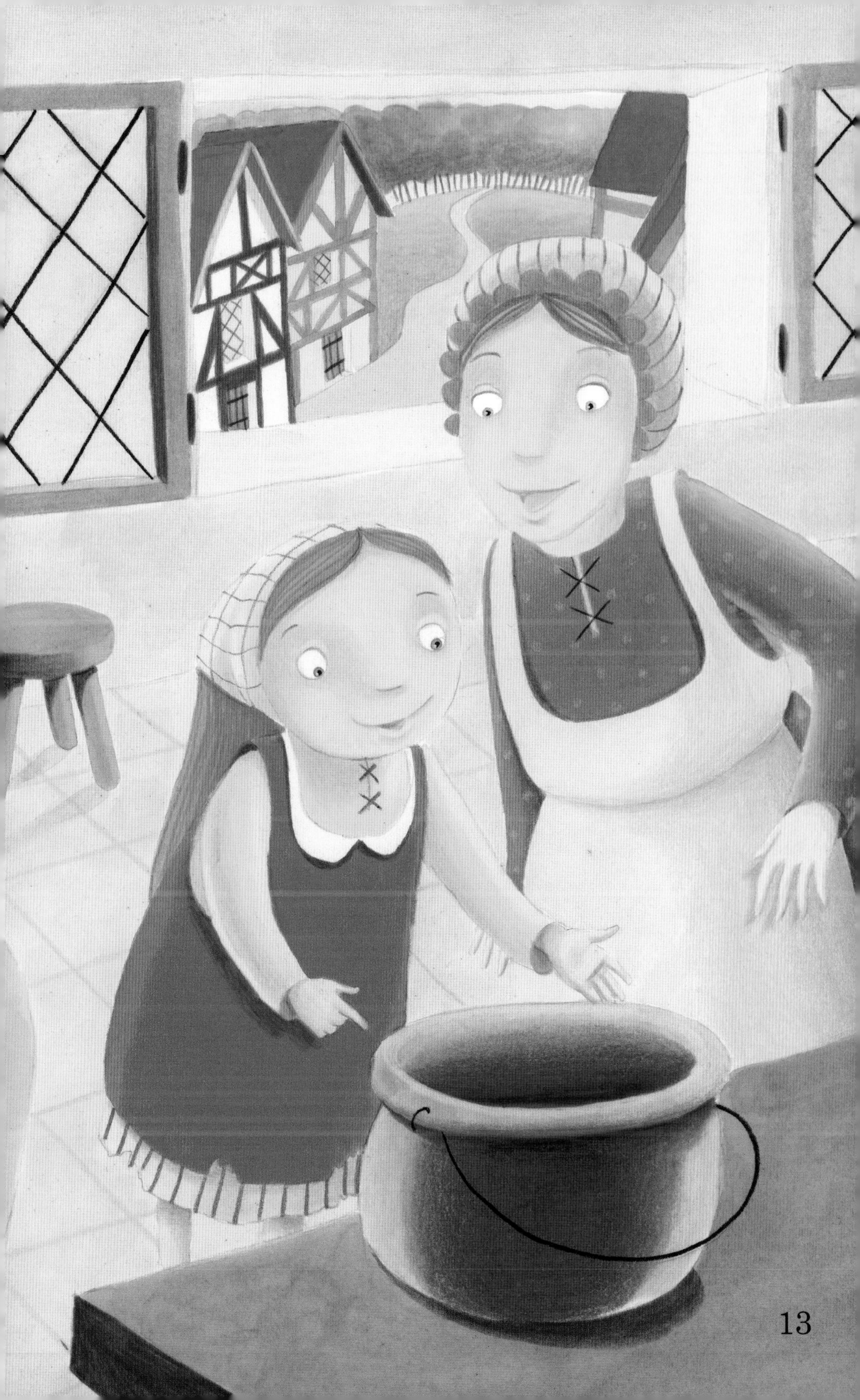

"Cook, little pot, cook," says the little girl's mother.

And the little pot cooks some porridge.

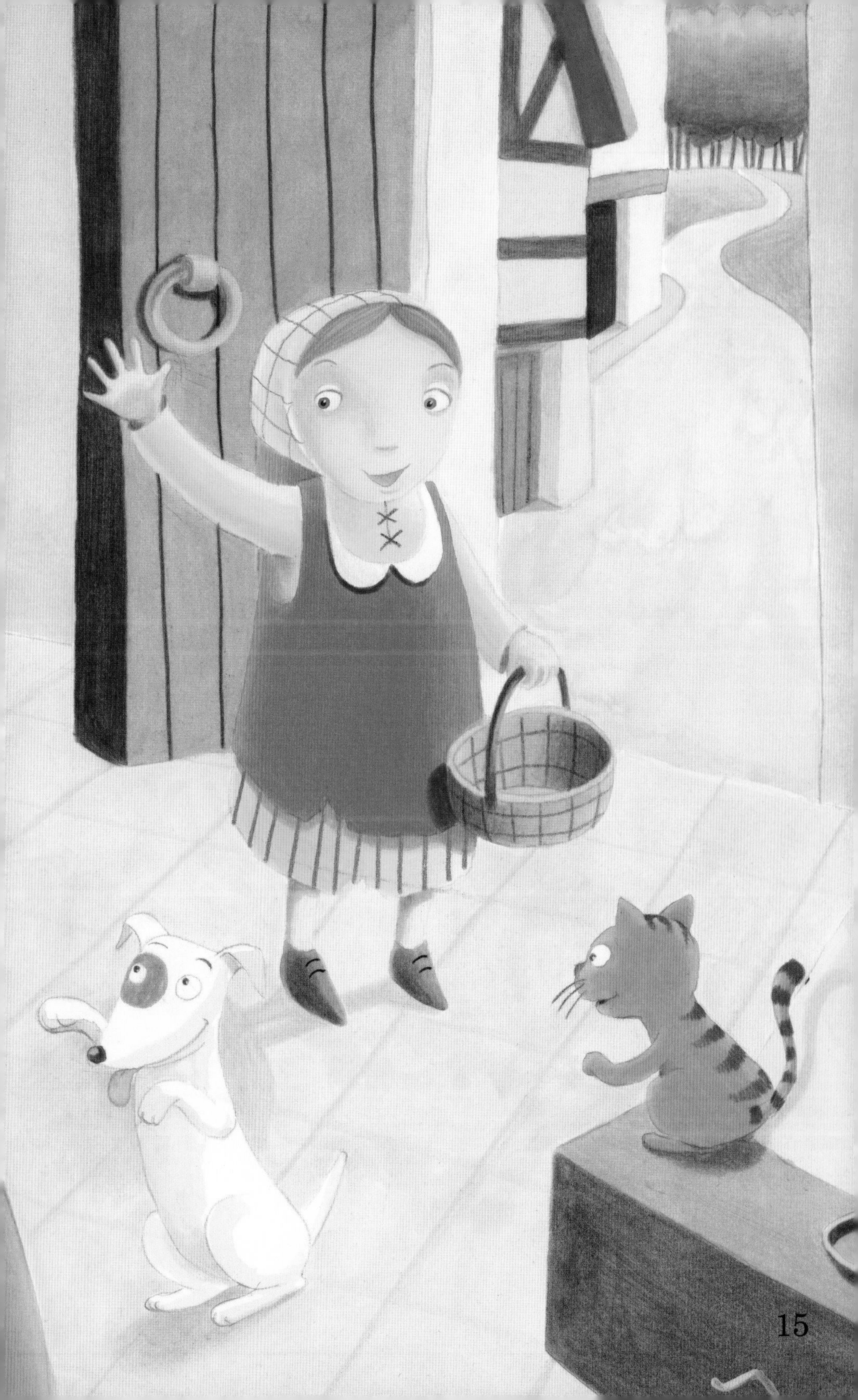

Now, there is lots of porridge in the kitchen.

But the magic porridge pot cooks and cooks.

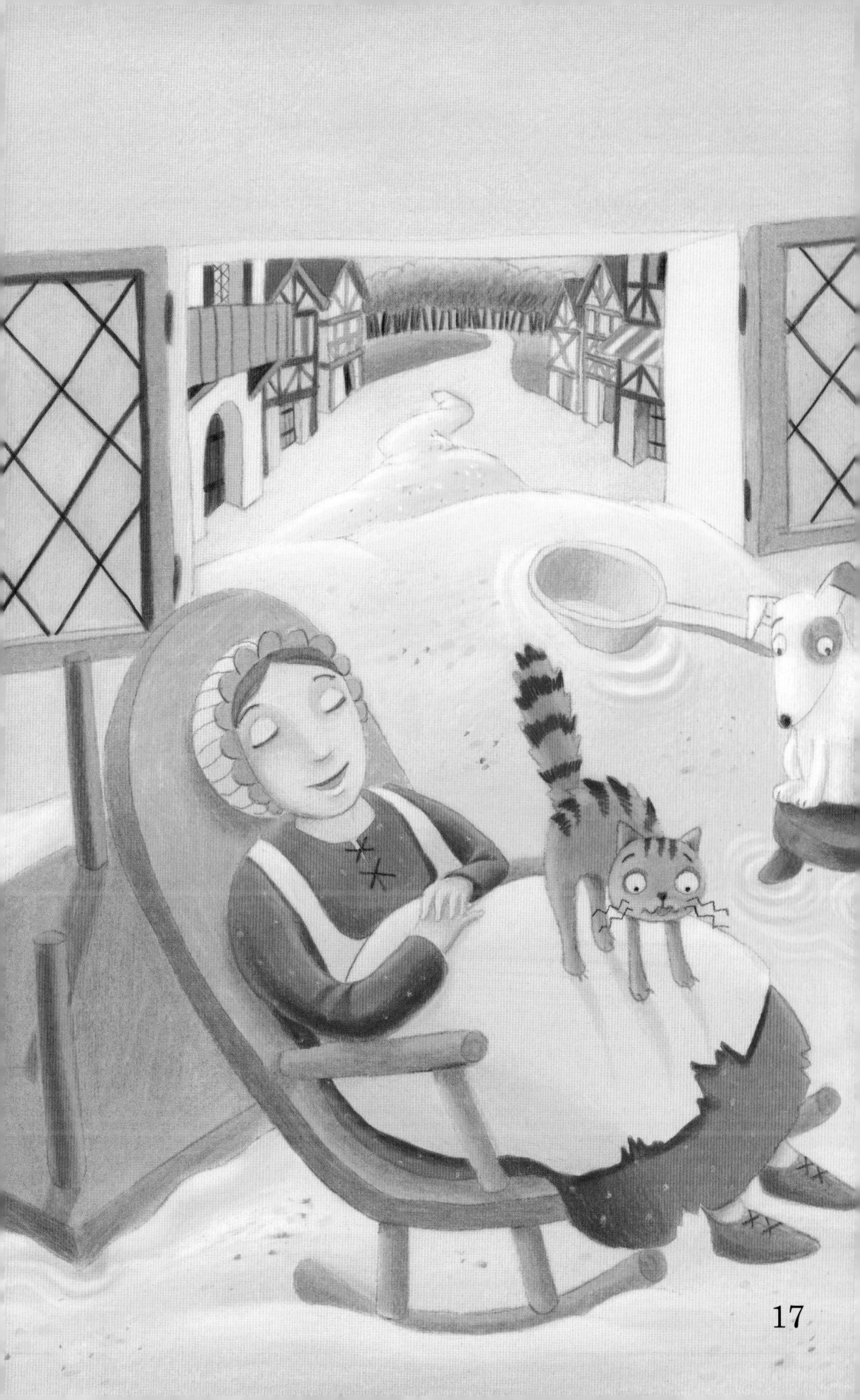

Now, there is lots of porridge in the house.

But the magic porridge pot cooks and cooks.

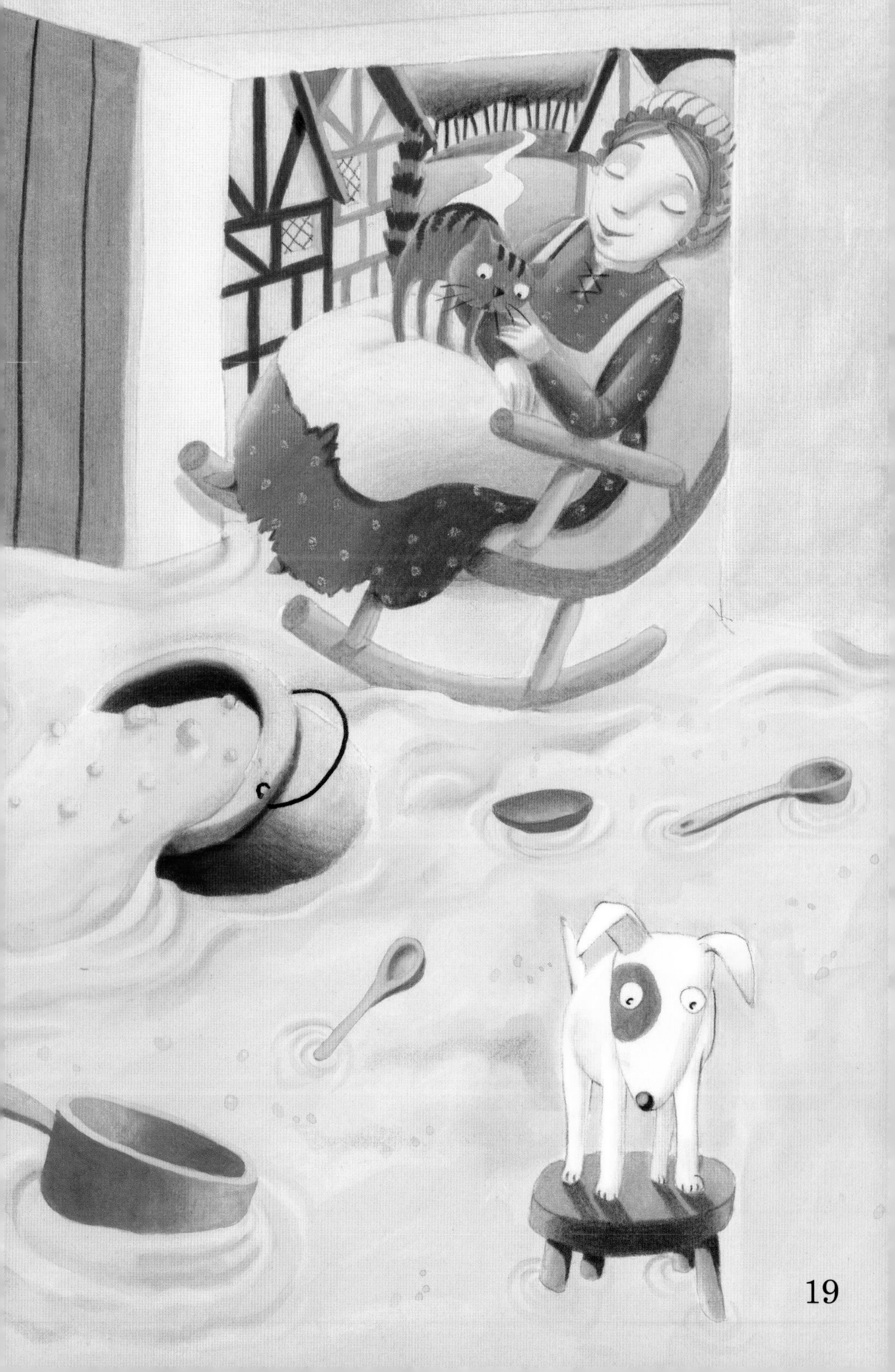

Now, there is lots of porridge in the street.

But the magic porridge pot cooks and cooks.

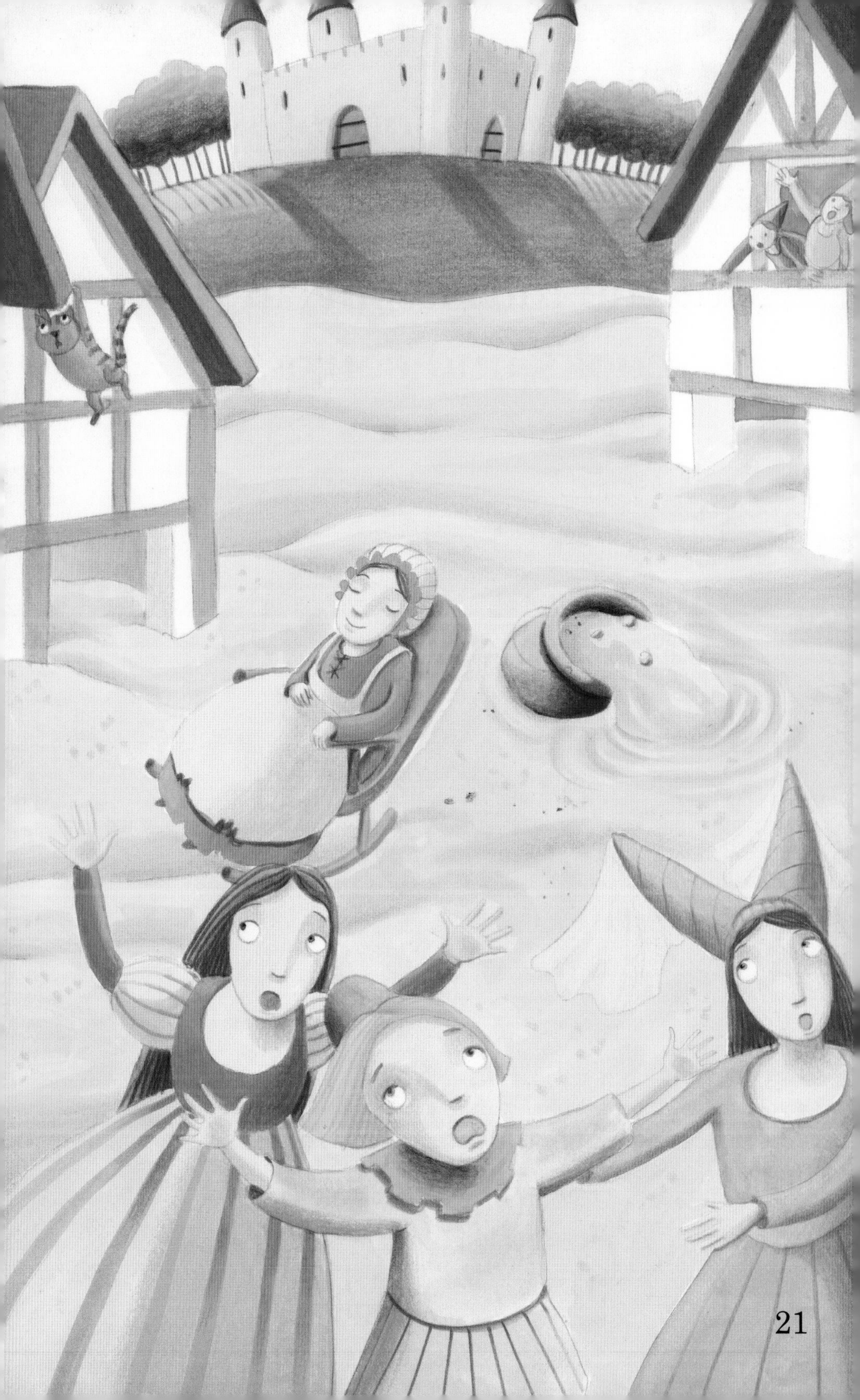

Now, there is lots of porridge in the town.

But the magic porridge pot cooks and cooks.

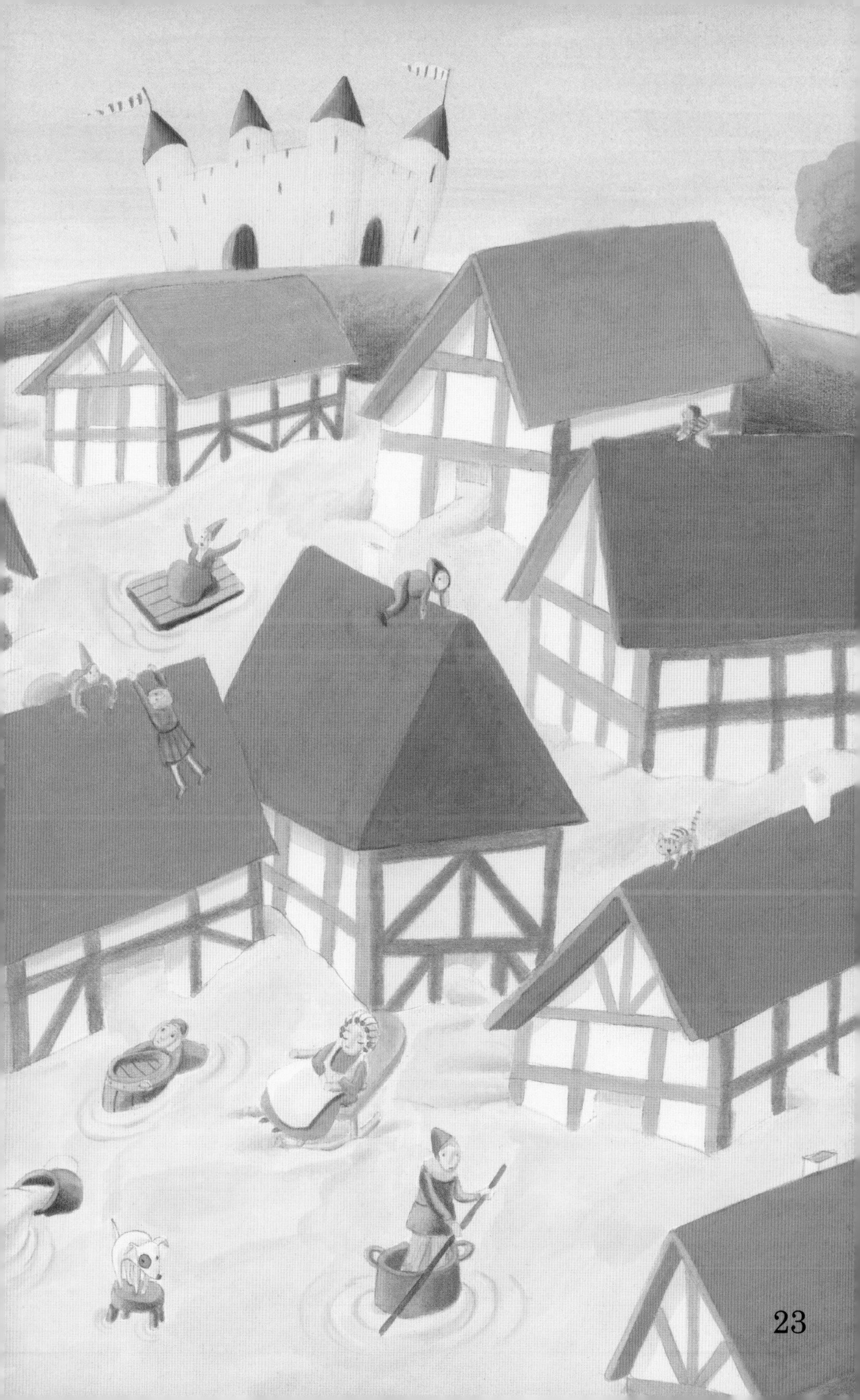

23

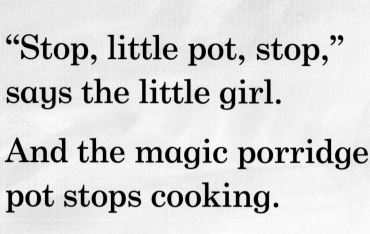

"Stop, little pot, stop,"
says the little girl.

And the magic porridge
pot stops cooking.

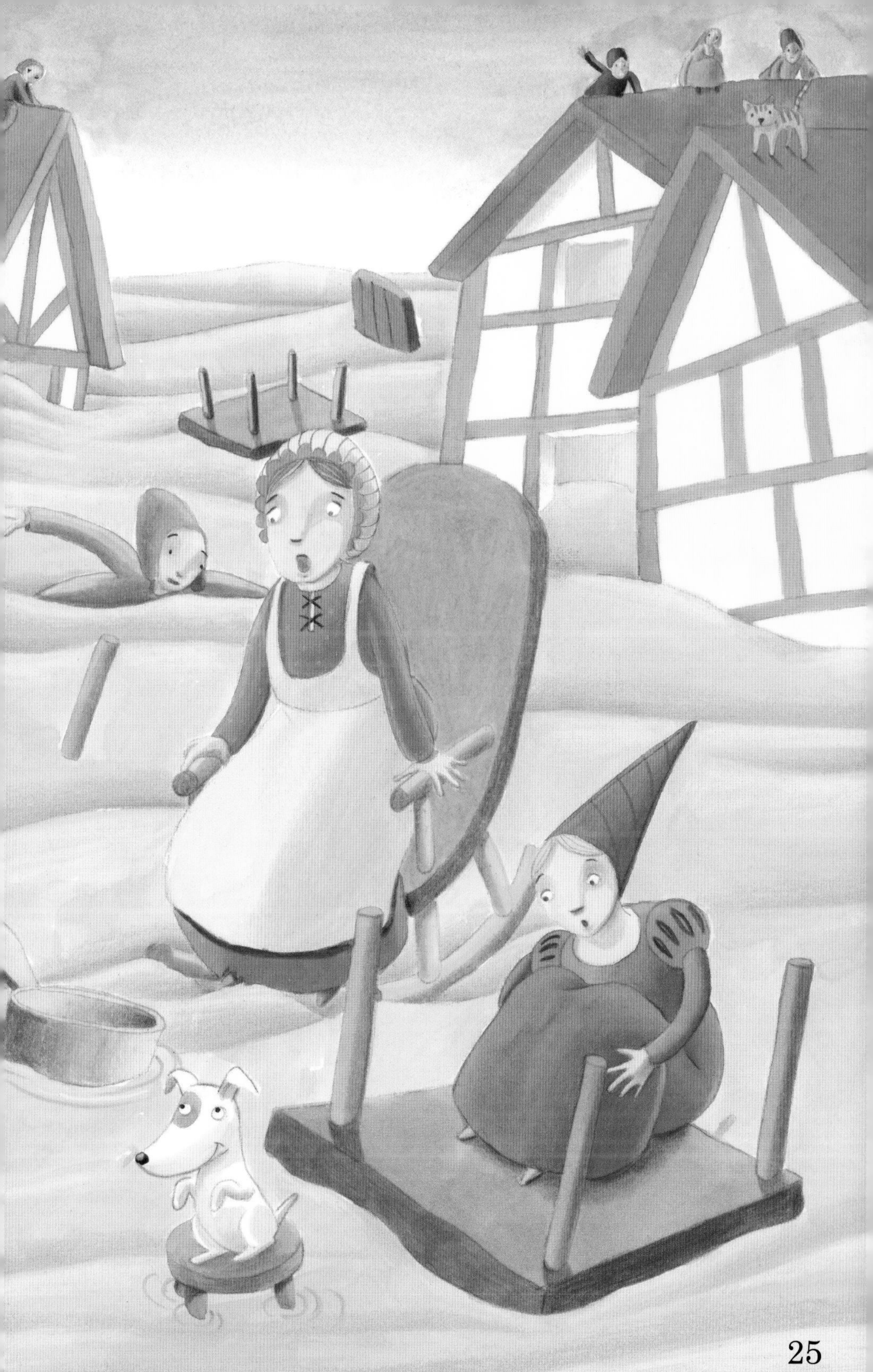

But now the people
are eating too
much porridge!

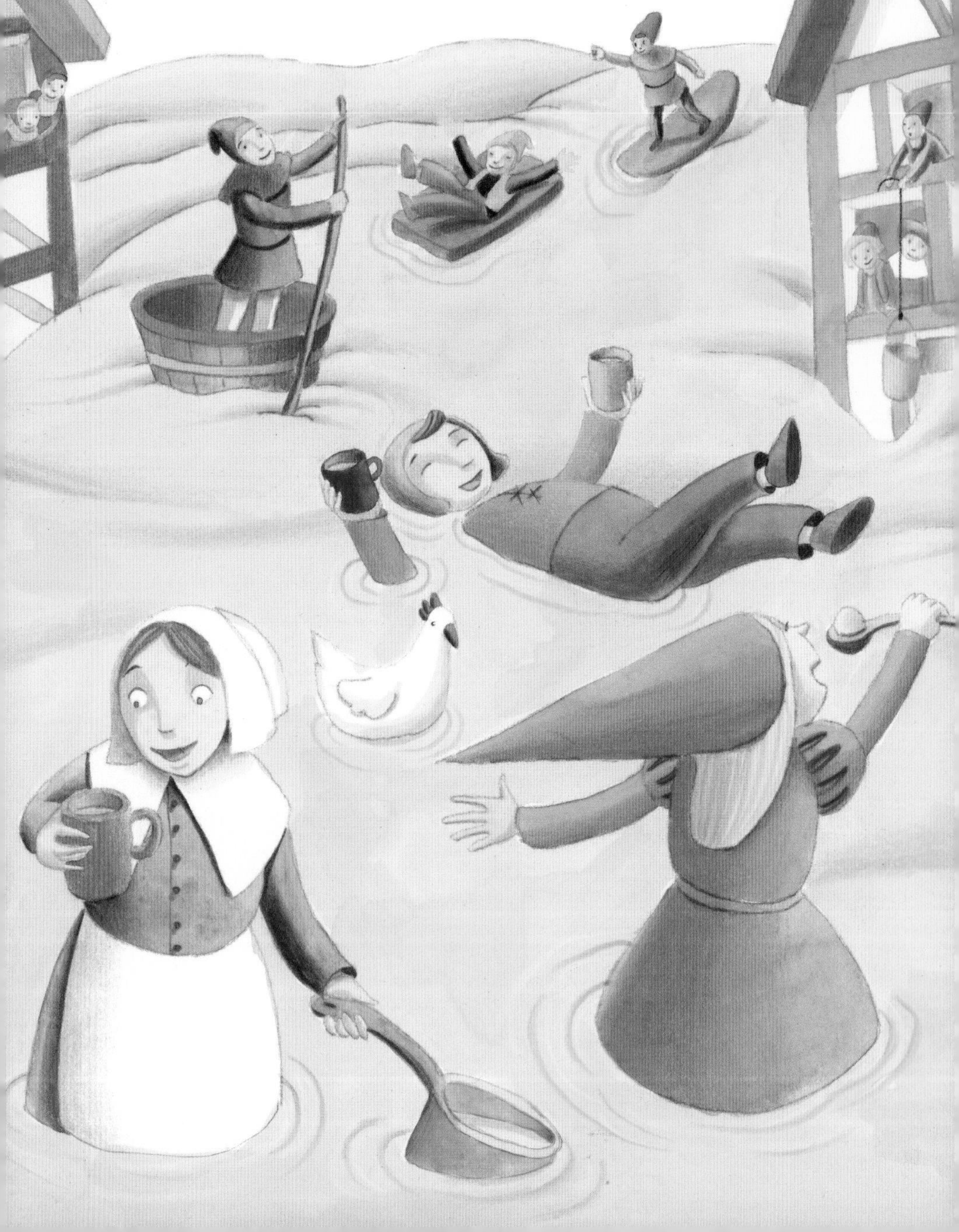

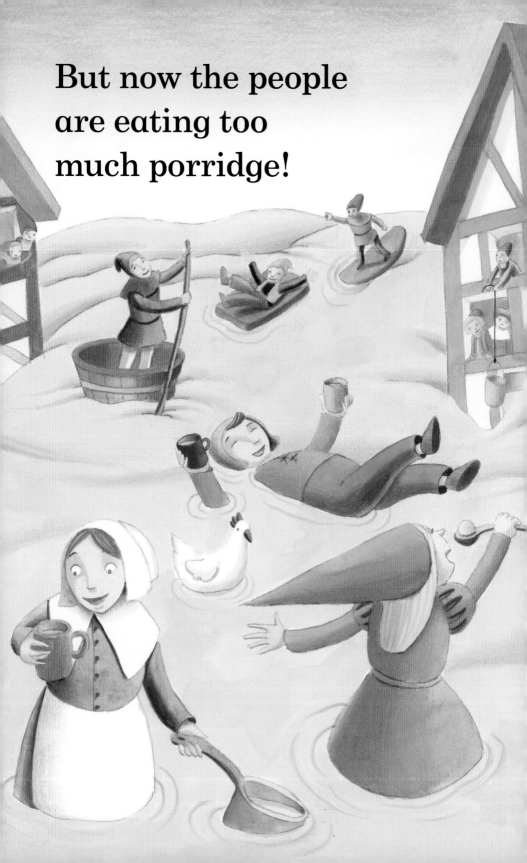

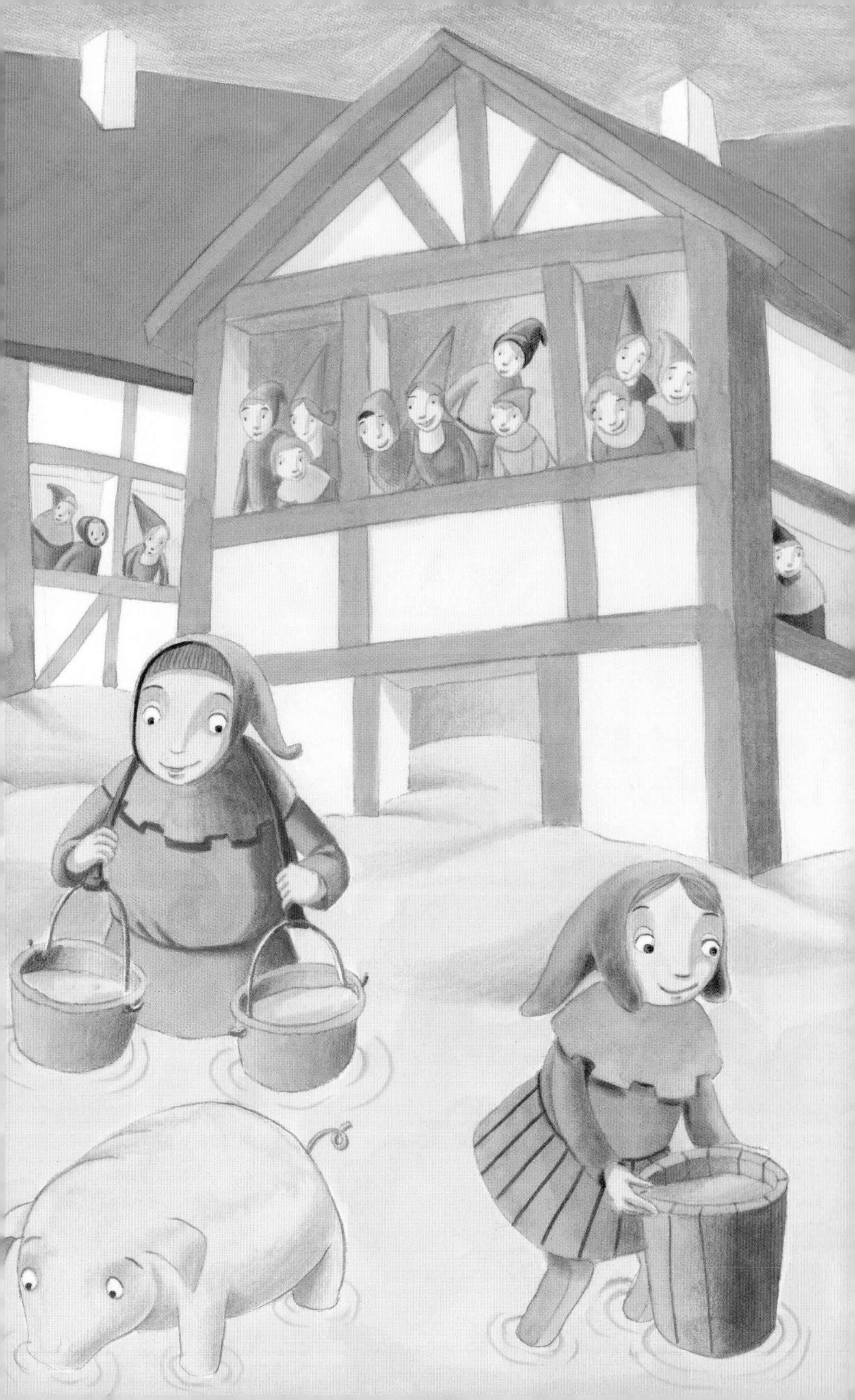

Activities

The key below describes the skills practiced in each activity.

Spelling and writing

Reading

Speaking

Critical thinking

Preparation for the Cambridge Young Learners Exams

1 Look and read.
Put a ✓ or a ✗ in the box.

1  This is the little girl. ✓

2  This is the
old woman. ☐

3  This is the mother. ☐

4  This is the
magic porridge pot. ☐

5  This is the town. ☐

2 **Look and read.**
Write yes or no. 📖 ✏️ ❂

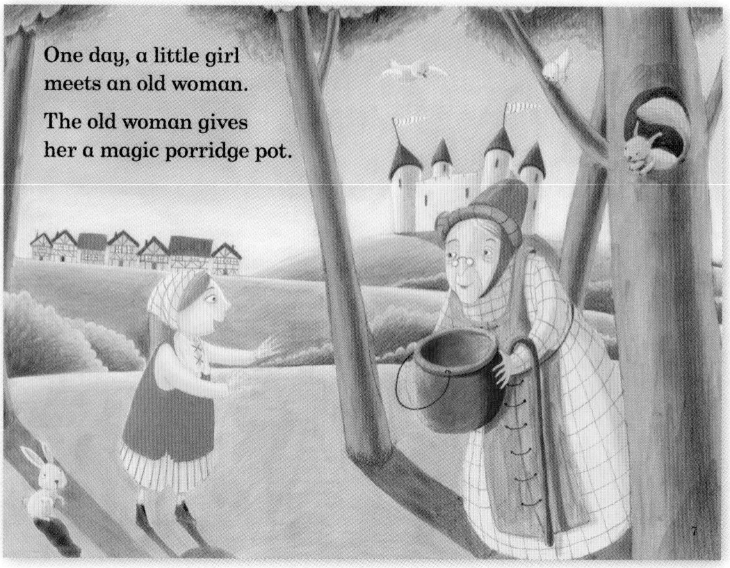

One day, a little girl meets an old woman.

The old woman gives her a magic porridge pot.

1 The little girl meets
an old woman.   ....yes....

2 The old woman gives
her an apple.   ....

3 The old woman talks
to the pot.   ....

4 The magic pot cooks a
lot of porridge.   ....

3 **Look at the pictures. Look at the letters. Write the words.**

1   t r e s t e

    s t r e e t

2   h o s e u s

    ___ ___ ___ ___ ___ ___

3   t m e o h r

    ___ ___ ___ ___ ___ ___

4   t o p

    ___ ___ ___

5   o w n t

    ___ ___ ___ ___

4 Work with a friend.
Talk about the mother's kitchen.

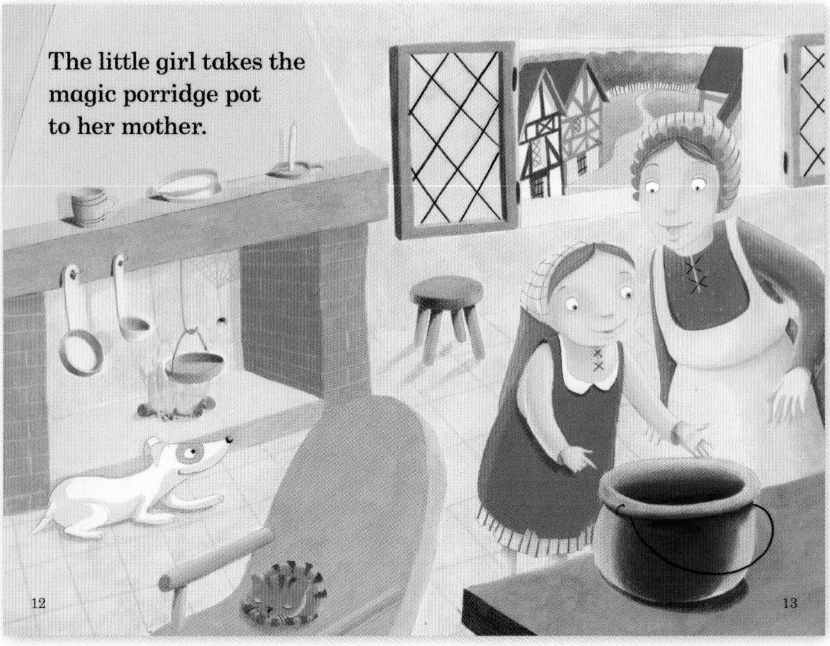

The little girl takes the magic porridge pot to her mother.

12   13

Example:

> *Has the mother got a green chair?*

> *Yes, she has got a green chair.*

5 **Look and read. Find the correct picture.** 📖

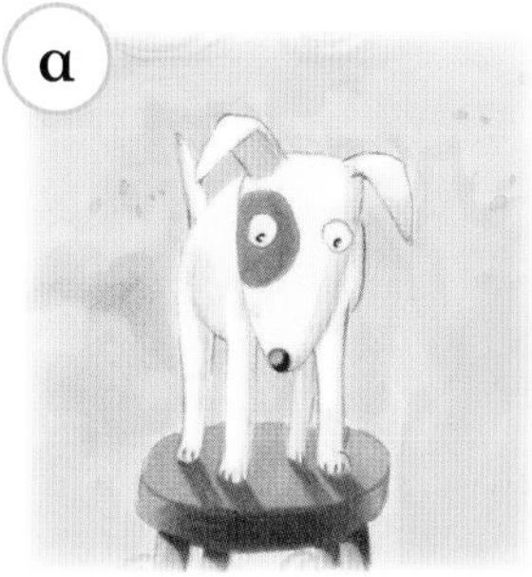

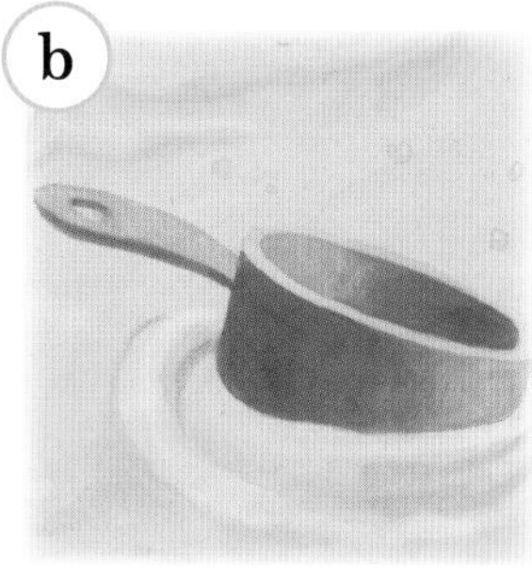

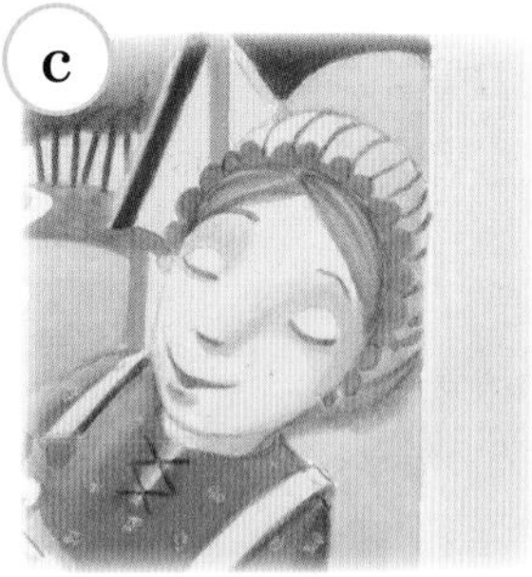

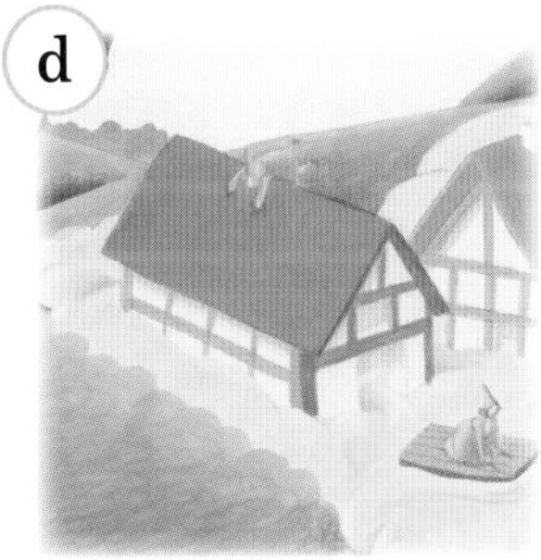

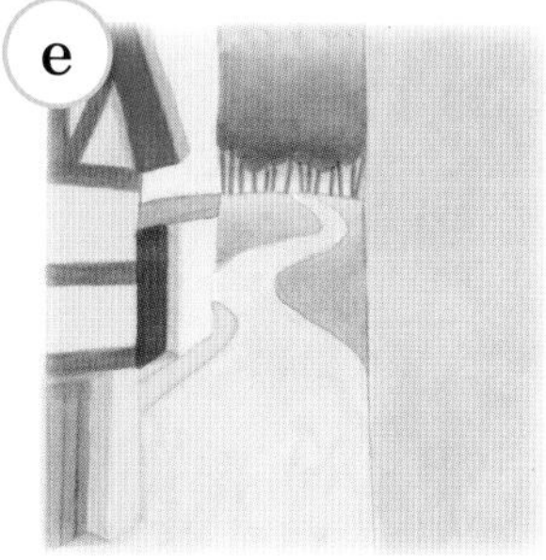

1 The mother is sleeping. ......C......

2 There is a house and street. ....

3 There is a dog. ....

4 There are two houses. ....

5 There is lots of porridge. ....

6 Circle the correct sentence.

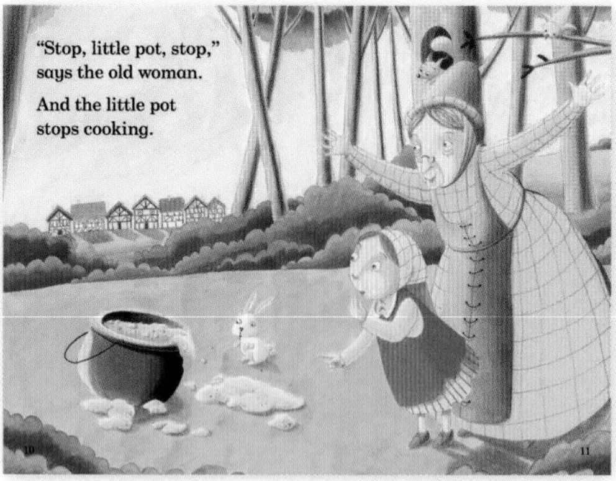

"Stop, little pot, stop," says the old woman.

And the little pot stops cooking.

1 a The little girl lives with her mother.

b The little girl lives with the old woman.

2 a The old man gives the girl a magic porridge pot.

b The old woman gives the girl a magic porridge pot.

3 a "Cook, little girl, cook," says the old woman.

b "Cook, little pot, cook," says the old woman.

7 Read and choose a word from the box. Write the correct word next to numbers 1—5.

kitchen   pot   mother   magic   porridge

The little girl takes the magic porridge pot to her ¹ __mother__ . "Cook, little ² _____ , cook," says the little girl's mother. And the little pot cooks some ³ _____ . Now, there is lots of porridge in the ⁴ _____ . But the ⁵ _____ porridge pot cooks and cooks.

8 Look and read.
Put a ✓ or a ✗ in the box.

Now, there is lots of porridge in the street.

But the magic porridge pot cooks and cooks.

1 Can you see a dog? ✓

2 Can you see a castle? ☐

3 Can you see the old woman? ☐

4 Can you see ten people? ☐

5 Can you see the magic porridge pot? ☐

9 **Write the missing letters.**

o o   r r   t t   e e

1 a li t   t le girl

2 a magic po _____ idge pot

3 Cook, little pot, c _____ k.

4 Now, there is lots of porridge
in the str _____ t.

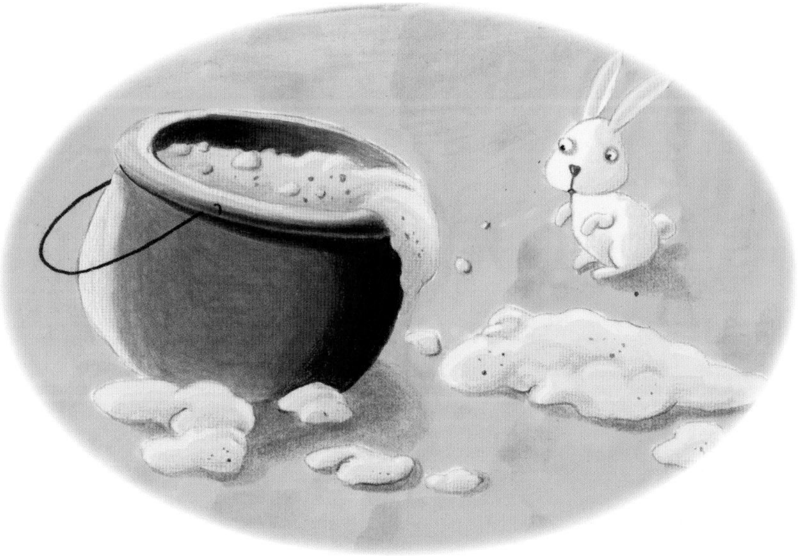

10 **Read this. Choose a word from the box. Write the correct word next to numbers 1—5.**

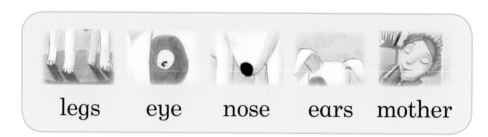

legs   eye   nose   ears   mother

I live with a little girl and her

1 ___mother___ . I have got four

2 _____ . I am white

and I have got a small brown

3 _____ . My

4 _____ is black. I can

hear very well with my two

5 _____ .

11 Write the answer.

1 Has the little girl got a brother?

No, she has not got
a brother.

2 Has the little girl got a mother?

3 Have the little girl and her mother got a cat?

12 **Ask and answer questions about the picture with a friend.**

Now, there is lots of porridge in the street.

But the magic porridge pot cooks and cooks.

1

Are the people happy?

No, they are not.

2 Is the mother running?

3 What are the children doing?

4 What are the people in the windows doing?

13 **Look and read.**
Write yes or no.

Now, there is lots of porridge in the kitchen.

But the magic porridge pot cooks and cooks.

1 The mother is sitting on a chair.   yes

2 The dog is on the mother.

3 The table is behind the green chair.

4 The magic porridge pot is in the kitchen.

5 The porridge is in the street.

14 **Look again at 13. Write *on*, *behind*, *next to*, or *in*.** 📖 ✏️

1 The dog is sitting .... on .... the little chair.

2 The table is .... the porridge pot.

3 The table is .... the mother.

4 The cat is .... the mother.

5 The mother is sleeping .... her kitchen.

15 **Ask and answer questions about the picture with a friend.**

1

What is the mother doing?

She is sleeping.

2 What is the magic porridge pot doing?

3 Is the dog happy?

4 Where is the porridge?

16 **Look at the picture and read the questions. Write one-word answers.**

Now, there is lots of porridge in the town.

But the magic porridge pot cooks and cooks.

1 Where is the little girl?

In the .... street ....

2 Where is the mother?

Sitting in her green ....

3 Where are the houses?

In the ....

4 How many people can you see?

....

17 **Look at the pictures. Read and circle the correct words.** 📖 ❓

1  The magic pot can **(understand people)** / **talk to people**.

2  The little girl says, **"Goodbye!"** / **"Stop, little pot, stop."**

3  The mother is **sleeping** / **happy**.

4  The dog is **sleeping** / **happy**.

5  The mother **sees** / **does not see** the porridge on the floor.

18 **Find the words.**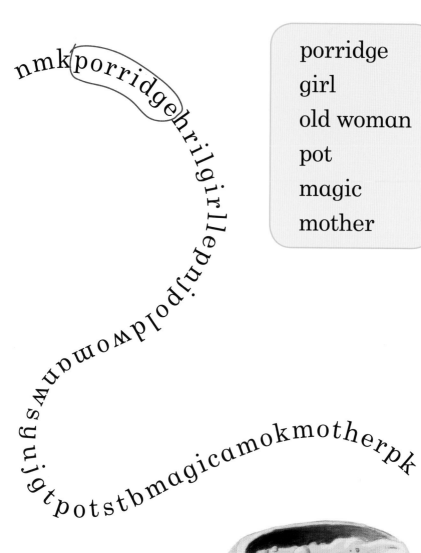

nmk(porridge)hrilgirllepnjpoldwoman swyjgtpotstbmagicamokmotherpk

porridge
girl
old woman
pot
magic
mother

19 Circle the correct word.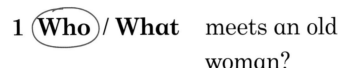

1 (Who) / What   meets an old woman?

2 **What / Where** does the magic porridge pot cook?

3 **What / Who**   does the little girl take the magic porridge pot to?

4 **Is / Are**   there lots of porridge in the house?

5 **Is / Are**   the people eating too much porridge?

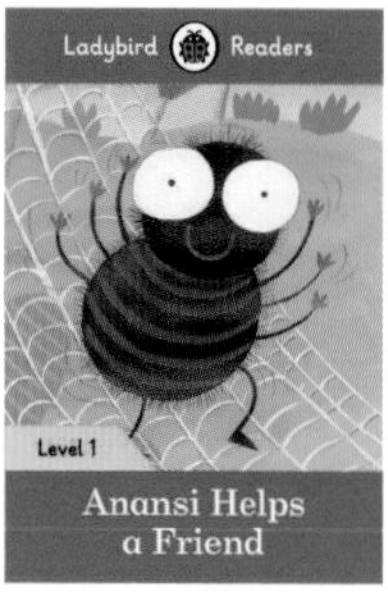

Level 1

**Anansi Helps
a Friend**

978–0–241–25409–7 ☐

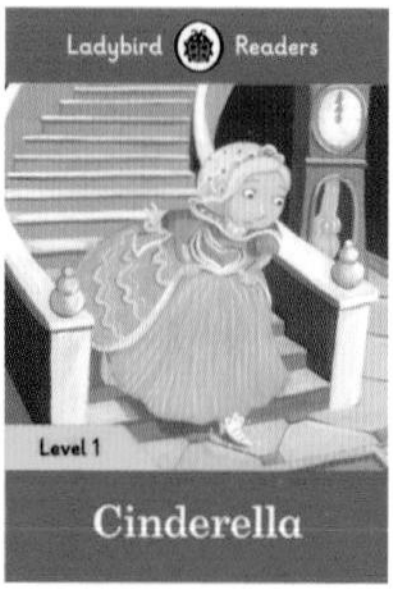

Level 1

Cinderella

978–0–241–25407–3 ☐

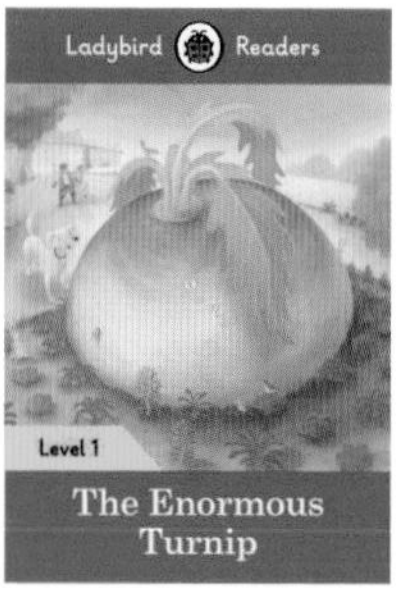

Level 1

**The Enormous
Turnip**

978–0–241–25408–0 ☐

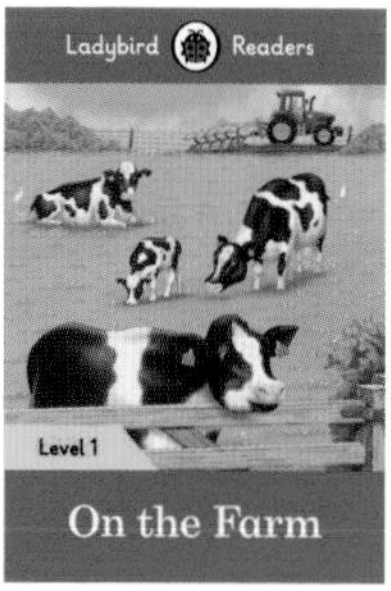

Level 1

On the Farm

978–0–241–25413–4 ☐

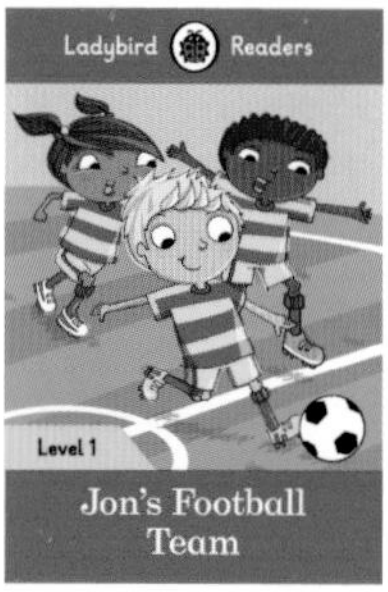

Level 1

**Jon's Football
Team**

978–0–241–25411–0 ☐

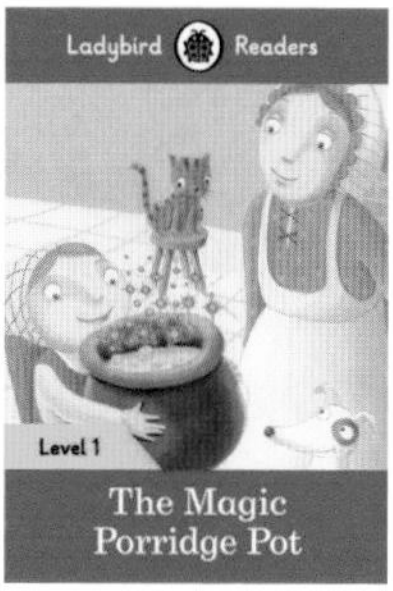

Level 1

**The Magic
Porridge Pot**

978–0–241–25406–6 ☐

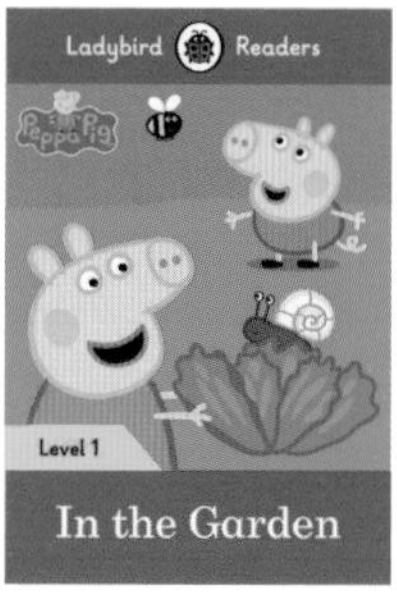

Level 1

In the Garden

978–0–241–26220–7 ☐

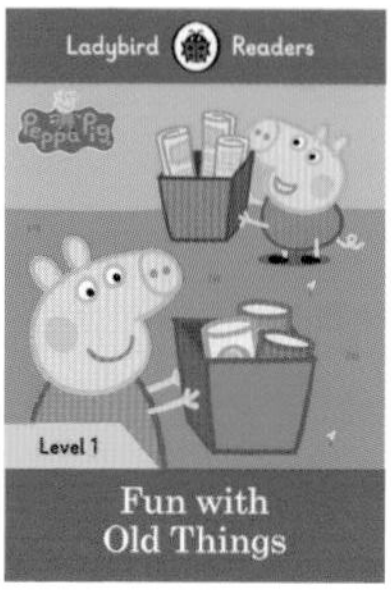

Level 1

**Fun with
Old Things**

978–0–241–26219–1 ☐

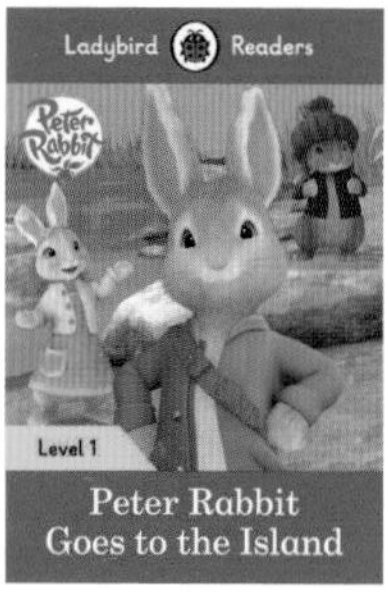

Level 1

**Peter Rabbit
Goes to the Island**

978–0–241–25415–8 ☐

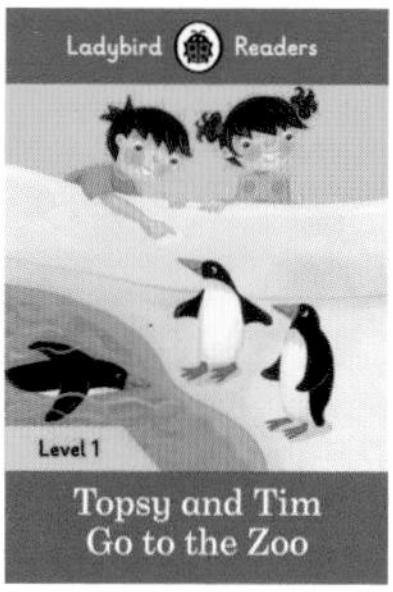

Level 1

**Topsy and Tim
Go to the Zoo**

978–0–241–25414–1 ☐

Now you're ready for Level 2!

Notes
CEFR levels are based on guidelines set out in the Council
of Europe's European Framework. Cambridge Young Learners
English (YLE) Exams give a reliable indication of a child's
progression in learning English.